Patrick Comes to Puttyville

Geoffrey Hayes

PATRICK COMES TO PUTTYVILLE

AND OTHER STORIES

HARPER & ROW, PUBLISHERS
New York, Hagerstown, San Francisco, London

JH

Library of Congress Cataloging in Publication Data
Hayes, Geoffrey.
    Patrick comes to Puttyville, and other stories.

    SUMMARY: Five stories relate the experiences of
Mama and Patrick Bear who leave their home in the
seafaring town of Catfish Bay and start a new life in
the country.
    [1. Bears—Fiction] I. Title.
PZ7.H31455Pat 1978   [Fic]   77–25668
ISBN 0–06–022266–2
ISBN 0–06–022267–0 lib. bdg.

for Mom
who read me stories
and Dad
who's been the Lantern Keeper all along

Contents

Patrick Comes to Puttyville

1

WHEN PATRICK was very young, he lived with his mother and father in a hut near the wharves in Catfish Bay. The hut was a dingy, low little dwelling, but Mama Bear did her best to keep it looking cozy and clean. Patrick's father, Old Pog, a mender of kettles and pans, had a tiny booth wedged between some ware-houses on the docks. But he was a rather unreliable sort. Instead of tending to his business, he could usually be found enjoying himself at one of the local taverns. In addition, he told lies, swiped things, and was forever having dealings with the police. So it surprised no one when he signed up as a sailor on a clipper ship to escape the law and was not heard from again.

For a long while after Old Pog went away, Mama Bear just sat round the house not doing much of anything. Occasionally, she'd take Patrick down to the beach. While he played in the sand, she would sit for hours staring across the water, hoping to see Old Pog return. But when he didn't, she decided to leave Catfish Bay and move to the country.

She put the little hut up for sale and held an auction to get rid of the furniture; then she packed the few belongings they had kept in baskets, bundles, and in her net-reticule.

Patrick was confused. "Why are we leaving, Ma?"

"We're going to begin a new life," she told him.

"But I just got started with *this* one!" said Patrick.

"Oh, you'll like the country," Mama Bear went on. "It's got open spaces, and trees, and—"

"Aren't we going to wait for Daddy to come back?"

"We don't need your father," Mama Bear said. "We're perfect the way we are."

On a bright afternoon in early summer, Patrick and Mama Bear gathered their bundles, left the hut, and walked to the end of the last pier. There, in a tiny houseboat adorned with colorful flags, lived Patrick's grandpa, Poopdeck. Captain Poopdeck looked very se-

rious when he saw them. "So, you're leaving after all!" he said, coming ashore.

"Yes, it's better this way," answered Mama Bear.

"You're welcome to stay with me, you know."

"We know," said Mama Bear, "and we appreciate the offer, but I think Patrick and I need a change."

"Whatever you say," replied Captain Poopdeck, taking Patrick in his arms and hoisting him over one shoulder. "I shall miss you."

"We'll miss you, too, Grandpa," said Patrick.

The three of them set off down the cobbled streets to the railway station at the end of town. Soon the cobblestones ended, the houses grew farther apart, and they came to a flat place of many trees. Patrick, who had never been this far, looked back to where Catfish Bay was spread round the ocean like a giant seashell.

"Things will be awfully lonesome on that old houseboat now," Captain Poopdeck sighed.

"Poppa, don't make this more difficult than it is," said Mama Bear. "Besides, you lead a busy life, and you have your cronies, so you've little to complain about."

"Aye, you're right. Well, if I do get lonely, I'll simply have to come visit *you*, won't I?"

"Oh, good!" exclaimed Patrick. "Will you come tomorrow?"

Captain Poopdeck chuckled. "No, not tomorrow, but soon—I promise."

He lowered Patrick from his shoulder, kissed him, scratched his ears, and drew him up close to his cheek. Patrick caught a whiff of saltwater, fur, and tobacco. "Ah, my pepper," Captain Poopdeck told him, "you have come to a turning of the tides. Now you're to play upon the bounds of a drier ocean . . . only don't forget your old grandpa, eh?"

Captain Poopdeck kissed Patrick twice more before setting him down. He kissed Mama Bear, held her paw, wished them both well, and hobbled slowly back to Catfish Bay without looking round. Mama Bear wiped her eyes on the sleeve of her coat.

Not far from the road, amid a tangle of bushes, stood the ticket office. It was a cramped, ramshackle building occupied by a whiskered old man with spectacles. "Howdy!" he called as Mama Bear and Patrick struggled over with their luggage. "What can I do for you?"

Puffing, Mama Bear set down a bundle, opened her reticule, and took out her purse. "I'd like two tickets to Puttyville, please: one child and one adult."

The old man moved behind him where various colored tickets wound with rubber bands lay stacked in cubbyholes. "Two to Flogersville, coming up."

"No, Puttyville," Mama Bear repeated.

"What's that?"

"*Puttyville* . . . not Flogersville."

"Well, make up your mind, would you?" retorted the old man, snatching a pile of yellow tickets. He started to remove a couple, but stopped and peered over his spectacles. "That's mighty far away; I'll have to charge you extra. . . . Sure you wouldn't rather go someplace closer?"

"Listen, just sell me the tickets," said Mama Bear impatiently. "I'm in no mood for back talk!"

"All right, you're the customer," said the old man. Then, turning to replace the remaining tickets, he muttered, "Grumpy bear!"

Patrick, who was studying a strange-looking pole next to the ticket office, began to feel anxious. "Maybe

it *is* too far, Ma. Maybe if we go Daddy will never be
able to find us."

Mama Bear's face grew stern. She took Patrick
aside and, lowering her voice, said, "Daddy has left.
He's not *coming* back. Besides, Puttyville will be
our new home . . . and we'll be happy there. You'll
see."

The old man squinted at the luggage. "I suppose
you'll be wanting help with them bags?"

"If you wouldn't mind," said Mama Bear.

Sighing, the old man came out of the ticket office, grasped a basket in each hand, and led them down a short incline to a quiet field. The train platform was a narrow structure with a red-shingled roof. Tufts of grass grew up through its wooden planks, and mosquitoes hummed about a faded sign which said: GREATMEAD-OWS.

"Will the train be long?" Mama Bear inquired.

The old man slid a watch fob from his trouser pocket, snapped it open, and replied, "Nope. She's running right on time . . . for a change. Further information's up there." And pointing to a small schedule hanging from the roof, he tipped his cap and sauntered back to his office, leaving Mama Bear and Patrick alone on the platform.

Patrick sniffed. This place was filled with queer smells; not the salty, fishy smell that rose from the sea; not the mixed smell of the shops and restaurants along the wharf; nor the musty, dark smell of the little hut where they used to live. Instead, the field had a warm smell—of hawthorn, damp leaves, rotten bark, and acorns.

They waited for what seemed a long time, until the sky turned a pale blue with pink at the edges. The evening brought out fireflies, hovering like stars over the thick grass, and from the trees came a *Cree cree!*

Cree cree! Patrick jumped. "Listen, Ma . . . what's that?"

"It's only crickets," she answered. "Those are bugs who sing all night by rubbing their hind legs together."

"Are they dangerous?"

Mama Bear laughed. "Not at all. The country is full of things that will seem strange until you get used to them. It's not a bit like Catfish Bay."

Patrick wanted to ask more about the country, but he heard a huffing noise in the distance. He could see a long stream of white smoke spiraling into the sky and a point of light growing steadily larger.

Squeezing his mama's paw, Patrick said, "I'm scared."

"There's nothing to be scared of," said Mama Bear.

Suddenly, the old man came running down the hill all out of breath, waving a lantern back and forth. He hurried over to a huge switch that stood next to the tracks. As the roar of the train engine grew louder, he jumped up and tugged the switch in the opposite direction, causing a section of track to slide over and lock together with the rest. The old man pulled a red bandana from his pocket and mopped his brow. "Whew! We almost had a wreck on our hands," he chuckled, and returned to his office. Mama Bear shook her head.

The black hulk of the engine came bursting through the trees with the engineer's face leaning out the window. He pulled a cord, the whistle screamed. With a throwing of throttle, a locking of wheels, and a hissing of steam, the *Puttyville Flyer* came to a resounding halt in front of the platform. It was shiny and colorful and all on wheels. "What a weird-looking thing," thought Patrick.

Patrick and Mama Bear gathered the luggage and hurried over to the first passenger car. The conductor came down the steps, tipped his cap, and said, "Evening, mum."

The steps were too high for Patrick, so the conductor lifted him aboard, and they went through a glass-paneled door into a car with rows of plush seats.

Patrick said, "Let's get one with a window."

"They all have windows. . . . How about this one?" Mama Bear said, pointing to a seat near the middle. Patrick scrambled up and looked through the glass while the conductor stored their bags in the overhead luggage rack.

The train was still making hissing noises, when they heard the conductor call, "All aboard! Next stop, Cattle Junction!"

With a rattle and a shake, the train came to life, moving slowly at first, then with accelerating speed. And the countryside whizzed past. "This is fun," said Patrick.

For about fifteen minutes he continued to stare out

the window, but since it was now almost night there wasn't much to see, and Patrick grew restless. He wandered down the aisle and discovered a drinking fountain at one end. It had a spigot and a dispenser with paper cups. Patrick poured himself a drink, then filled another cup to take to his mama. But when he walked back the train rounded a curve, making the car tilt. Patrick slipped and spilled the cup of water on an old gentleman who snorted, "Children!"

"Oh, sorry," said Patrick.

"Patrick!" called Mama Bear. "Come here and sit still!"

"I was just trying to get you some water," Patrick explained as he climbed into his seat.

"I know, but you mustn't bother the other passengers." She unfastened her reticule, dug about, and brought out a box of Uneeda biscuits and some cheese.

"Oh, boy! A snack!"

When the conductor came to collect the tickets, Mama Bear offered him a slice of cheese.

"Thanks, mum," he said, "only it wouldn't look proper while I'm on duty."

Patrick noticed that the conductor had a stack of pillows under one arm. "Can we get one?" he asked.

"Of course," said Mama Bear. "Two, please. . . . How much is that?"

"No charge," replied the conductor, handing them the pillows.

Patrick put his behind his head. "What is Puttyville like, Ma?"

"Oh," said Mama Bear, "it's a nice, quiet town in a valley surrounded by meadows. Once, before any buildings were there, it was supposed to be a wild place where wizards walked and worked their magic; but for as long as I can recall it's been lovely and rather ordinary."

"You mean you've been there already?" cried Patrick.

"Yes, every summer when I was a girl I used to go visit my grandmother. She owned the house at the edge of the forest where we're going to live. She was an odd old bear. At times she could be extremely grouchy—she didn't have much use for other people—but she liked me, and when she died several years ago she left me the house."

"Why haven't we been there before?" Patrick asked.

"I wanted to move right off . . . but your father wouldn't hear of being stuck in the country. He was too fond of the different people coming and going in Catfish Bay, but I think the country is just as exciting in its own way, and a lot less noisy."

"Did you ever go into the forest?"

"Yes, indeed! Grandmother often sent me there to pick berries. Oh, it was wonderful!"

"Is there an ocean in the forest?"

"No, only little places of water. The ones that are round are called lakes, and the ones that are thin and go on and on are called rivers."

Mama Bear told Patrick what the river is saying as it gurgles and sputters, winding its way down the mountains, why dew is on the morning grass, and why cobwebs are sticky. She explained where the badger hides, where the bees fly, and how the mother fox nestles her pups in her wild, red fur, while the father fox, using stealth and cunning, prowls for hens' eggs for dinner.

By now, all the lights in the train had been turned down and people were going to sleep. "How long before we get there, Ma?"

"We'll be there when you wake up in the morning," said Mama Bear.

"Oh, I'm not going to sleep," Patrick replied. "I'm going to stay awake all night."

"Suit yourself," Mama Bear said.

Pressing his face to the window, Patrick tried counting the stars, only the train was moving too fast. He eventually grew tired and pulled the shade down. Snuggling close to his mama, Patrick said,

"Tell me the part about the father fox again."

So Mama Bear did, and by the time she had finished, Patrick was sleeping.

2

Patrick awoke to gray light seeping under the window shade and the *clickety-clack* of the wheels below. Mama Bear was still asleep, so he pulled up the shade, hoping the light would wake her, but she didn't stir.

They were traveling through a rich green land of shady forests and misty hills. Here and there, shepherds were leading their sheep out to graze. A few paused to wave back at Patrick. Then the shepherds were gone, more trees whizzed by, and a farm appeared with cows and horses.

Soon the train slowed down and stopped at a small station consisting of a water tower and a dairy farm. Workmen came from the dairy lugging giant tanks of milk which they lifted onto the train with a loud clatter.

The noise woke Mama Bear. "We're nearly there," she said. "This is the last stop before Puttyville." Rummaging inside her reticule, she brought out apples and granola for breakfast.

In no time the train was on its way, skirting broad

meadows dotted with clusters of blue columbine. When it entered a brick tunnel, the *clickety-clack* of the wheels became a dull *thumpety-thump*, there was a brief spell of darkness, and then they burst into the sunlight again.

Across a great blue river, Puttyville's houses hugged the hillside, their peaked roofs and gables shining bright as marble in the warming sun!

The train crossed the river and pulled smoothly into the station where groups of people milled about, waiting to board, waving to arriving passengers, or getting ready to unload the boxcars. Patrick was startled when everyone rose at once and clogged the aisle, pushing to get off.

"Let's wait until everyone leaves," said Mama Bear.

"But what if the train starts up again while we're still on it?" said Patrick.

"Don't worry, we have plenty of time."

After most of the people were gone, the conductor came by and helped Mama Bear remove their stuff from the luggage rack. "Got any cheese left?" he asked hopefully.

"No," said Mama Bear. "Sorry."

They left the crowded station and headed toward Puttyville's main street. At the entrance of the town was a park with a bandstand, and across the way, buildings rose against the slope of the valley. Patrick

17

marveled at how clean the shops were; they were of different heights and had sparkling windows with fancy lettering advertising everything from books and clothing to handmade furniture. He wanted to stop at every window, but Mama Bear bustled ahead. "Wait, Ma. . . ."

"I'll bring you downtown later," she said. "First we must unpack the luggage and get settled."

She turned up one of the hills. It was so steep that they had to rest several times before they reached the top; but finally they came to a level area where a sign on a tall pole read: TRUMBLE STREET. Being the last

block before the woods, it was mostly dirt, with flat rocks and patches of grass. Rows of solid wooden houses faced one another. Some had gardens in front, enclosed by picket fences, others simply opened off the street. The neat, brown house on the corner next to the vacant lot was their new home.

As they approached, they heard screaming and banging coming from within. Mama Bear, hurrying forward, went up the stoop and rang the doorbell. The ruckus continued, so Mama Bear rang the bell again. Then a voice said, "Someone's at the . . . listen, watch it . . . quit that!"

Mama Bear rang a third time.

"Just shut up!" screamed the voice. "Behave yourself!"

There was a clicking of locks, and the door opened slightly, revealing a woman with unkempt hair who held a broom in one hand. "Yeah? Whadda ya want?" she asked harshly.

"I am Mrs. Pog!" remarked Mama Bear. "And this is my house. Who are *you*?"

With that, the woman flung the door open all the way and did a curtsy. "Well, ex-*cuse* me! I had no idea you were arriving so soon. I'm Mrs. Rinko, the lady you wrote to about tidying the place up a bit."

"Indeed!" said Mama Bear, pushing forward.

She and Patrick entered a low-ceilinged hallway with

19

a staircase to one side. On the stairs, two chubby little girls with greasy dresses were hitting one another.

"Stop that!" Mrs. Rinko yelled.

One of the girls grabbed a Yo-Yo and swung it at the other, who tumbled off the steps and scurried into the parlor.

Mama Bear looked disapprovingly at the freshly painted walls which were smudged with fingerprints and marked with crayon drawings of an elephant and a giraffe. "It doesn't look like you've done a very good job getting this place clean," she said.

Mrs. Rinko grinned broadly and curtsied again. "Beg pardon, ma'am. The painters *were* here yesterday, but my little tykes just can't keep their hands to themselves. They require such looking after, I haven't found the time . . ."

The two little girls came out of the parlor at top speed, falling all over each other on the hall carpet.

"Hanna! Maria! Stop this at once! I want you to say hello to Mrs. Pog here. And mind your manners!"

Hanna and Maria stopped squealing and stared at Mama Bear. But they didn't say, "Hullo." They just looked at her in a curious and disgusted manner. Then they saw Patrick standing shyly in a corner. "Oh, lookit *him*!" exclaimed Maria.

They ran over and started pinching and poking at him. "Lookit his funny ears!" Hanna said.

Maria had gone behind and was pointing to Patrick's
tail. "Hah!" she chortled. "He's got fur on his butt!"

Patrick slapped her hand. "Leave me be!" he cried.

"Oh, Mummy! He hit me!" Maria screeched. "That
nasty bear hit me!"

Mama Bear clicked her tongue and glanced into the
kitchen. There were her grandmother's best china
dishes piled on the edge of the sink. They were smeared
with leftover food, and a couple even had chips in
them. "That does it!" said Mama Bear. "I want you out
of my house this instant!"

Mrs. Rinko looked dazed. "But . . . but begging your pardon, ma'am . . ."

"Go on, get! And take your obnoxious daughters with you!"

"Well, I never!" declared Mrs. Rinko. ". . . Uh, where's my pay?"

Mama Bear snapped open her purse and took out some change. Shoving it into Mrs. Rinko's hand, she said, "Here! You're lucky I don't smack you all with the broom!"

Mrs. Rinko sniffed and marched away, dragging her two offspring by the braids. At the door, Maria spun round and stuck her tongue out at Patrick.

"Well, I hope that's the last we'll be seeing of *those* pigs!" said Mama Bear as she shut the door. "How unpleasant!"

Things seemed remarkably quiet without Hanna and Maria screaming. For a few minutes Patrick and Mama Bear stood in the hallway enjoying the feel of their new home. Smiling, Mama Bear sighed, "Ah, it's good to be back in the old house. But come, we've got work to do!"

Patrick helped bring in the luggage; then, while Mama Bear washed the dishes and scrubbed the walls, he went exploring. Downstairs was the kitchen with its pantry, its formidable iron stove, and a dining nook in one corner. Off the hall was a snug parlor with a fireplace. Patrick thought it would be nice to lie in front of it in the winter. But the furniture was old-fashioned and musty, and Patrick did not like it; so he went to see if the upstairs was any better. Upstairs were two bedrooms. One of them had a sloping ceiling and a double-paned window overlooking the backyard.

Opening the window, Patrick discovered that the roof of the kitchen was right underneath. He crawled out, sat upon it, and looked at the yard. Patrick thought what fun it would be to play in the overgrown grass, so much nicer than the cobbled streets of Catfish Bay. "This is going to be *my* room," he decided as he clambered back inside, "so I can come and sit on this roof whenever I want."

Later, when he went to sleep in his new room with his toys, his brush, and clothes still packed in bundles about him, he thought, "These are all my things, and we've traveled all this way together, and when I open them up I'll have a part of Catfish Bay here with me."

Morning sunlight streaming through the window woke Patrick, and for a few minutes he couldn't remember where he was. The mattress felt strangely soft and the sheets were cold, but when he noticed his toys and the smell of fresh paint, he scrambled out of bed and hurried downstairs where Mama Bear was frying pancakes. Already the house was beginning to seem like home.

3

As the weeks passed, Mama Bear hung paintings of starlit nights and wild flowers in the hall. She bought slipcovers for the parlor furniture, a bureau for Patrick's room, and new pans and bowls for the kitchen. In the mornings after breakfast, Mama Bear would take down her red-covered recipe book and study the different sections to decide what to cook. She made wonderful stews from vegetables and herbs, salads and omelettes, and pies and cookies.

Patrick always got excited when he saw the kitchen with flour all round because it meant Mama Bear was baking something. On the table there would be waxed paper, and on top of the waxed paper a lump of white dough which looked like nothing in particular, but out of which Mama Bear could make piecrust or toasted cookies.

On a pie day, Patrick sat at the high, wooden table and plucked stems from the berries they had bought in town. He dropped them into a saucepan which was set over the fire to simmer. A syrup oozed from the berries, then the syrup went into the piecrust, and Mama Bear cut narrow strips of dough to lay over the top.

Sometimes she'd let Patrick roll the dough out. He enjoyed using the rolling pin and sprinkling flour until it was all over the table, the utensils and the floor.

Whenever Mama Bear had her back turned, Patrick tore off a piece of dough and popped it into his mouth, and she often wondered why there wasn't enough to make strips.

If she felt ambitious Mama Bear made three pies at once: a peach, an apple, and a berry, and slid them all into the oven side by side. As they were cooking, the fragrance of the different flavored pies permeated the kitchen and got mixed together in Patrick's nose, like a tree with different kinds of fruit on it.

If it was a cookie day, Mama Bear brought out her assortment of tin cookie cutters. When Patrick pressed them into the dough, patterns began to appear: stars and bells and circles and little men. And afterwards when they were laid on the pan, there was a whole selection of colored sprinkles to put on top. When they were baked, Patrick and Mama Bear always ate them up at once—every last crumb—as they sat drinking tea in the warm, moist kitchen.

In the afternoons, if the weather was nice, Patrick and Mama Bear went to the park. They sat on the lawn watching people strolling about the green or resting on benches beneath the trees. Some of the people were in a hurry and walked right through, looking neither right nor left. Others seemed as if they were going to be there all day. There were women with fine bonnets and elegant gowns, storekeepers taking a rest from work,

and fat men who stretched out lengthwise on a bench or on a slope and turned their faces to the sun.

But children came to the park, too. And Old Wolfgang the Balloon Man. He stood next to the bandstand with his gold helium pump and innumerable balloons, singing:

"Buy a balloon, buy a balloon!
Bright as the sun and round as the moon!"

He sold balloons to children and parents and nursemaids, and sometimes even to old ladies. Every time Patrick saw Old Wolfgang, he would beg Mama Bear

for money to buy a balloon, a red one; and if she agreed, he would run with his balloon all over the spaces and hills of the park. But if other children tried to follow him, Patrick became shy and hurried back to Mama Bear. "That's all right," she'd say. "You've done enough running. We'll just watch for a while." On the finest days, Patrick would look up to see the park covered by a tent of balloons of all colors, bobbing delicately in the summer air.

Patrick asked Mama Bear to take him into the forest, to show him where she had picked berries as a little girl. She always said, "Soon," then seemed to forget all about it. Patrick would have loved to go exploring among the massive, ruddy-brown trees, which grew from the ground as if they were an extension of the earth, but Mama Bear had forbidden him to enter the forest without her.

Each night she sat at his bedside and told him woodland stories. Patrick especially loved the part about the father fox, and he would ask Mama Bear to tell it to him time and again. But always when she'd finished, Patrick would say, "We don't need a father fox, do we? We're perfect the way we are." And Mama Bear would smile, plant a kiss on his forehead, and bustle off to her own room.

As he was going to sleep, Patrick heard the call of the old hoot owl, and from his window saw a long, swift streak of dark wings. The round hedgehogs lay snoring in their holes, and the fox sang freely as it padded over the forest's leafy floor—"on its way to search for hens' eggs," thought Patrick. Then he tried to picture his own father. But with each night his memory of his father faded until all he could recall was an aroma of cigar smoke, and it seemed as though his father was only a ghost made of smoke. Heavy with sleep, Patrick would squeeze into his pillows and mumble drowsily, "We don't need a father fox. . . ."

4

Toward the end of summer, Patrick noticed a sharpness in the air as the long days grew slowly shorter. The change of seasons had been slight in Catfish Bay, for there the weather was always damp and gloomy with occasional spells of sun—in the winter it just rained more—but Puttyville was different. Patrick saw the trees turn faintly gray, and watched the clouds moving faster over the hills.

People began to repair the shutters, paint the fences, and clean the chimneys of their homes. Several bakery shops, closed during the month of August, now reopened with enticing assortments of pastry. When Patrick and Mama Bear went downtown they frequently saw HELP WANTED signs in the windows. Mama Bear would pause and stare at the signs with an anxious look on her face.

One day Patrick was in the backyard trying out his new slingshot on some squirrels when he heard the gate click, meaning Mama Bear had returned from town. Forgetting about the squirrels, Patrick ran over to her. "Hullo, Ma! What did you bring me?"

But Mama Bear's arms were empty. Sitting down on the swing, she said, "Nothing this time. I'm afraid we are running out of money."

"Then we'd better find some right away," Patrick said.

Mama Bear smiled, but she did not seem very happy. "Patrick, I know how to get some money; you see I . . . I've taken a job at one of the bakery shops."

"A job?" cried Patrick. "Oh, boy! When do we start?"

Now Mama Bear laughed. "No, Patrick, you don't understand. This job is just for me; anyway, it's time you started school."

"School? What's that?"

"It's a place where you learn things."

"Can't I just learn things at home?"

Mama Bear lifted Patrick onto her lap and gently swung him back and forth. "But I can't leave you alone all day. At school there will be lessons and games to keep you occupied and other children to play with."

"No!" said Patrick, sliding off her lap. "I don't want to!"

"Now, Patrick, be reasonable. Sooner or later you have to make some friends."

"I already have a friend," said Patrick. "—You!"

The next morning, before it was completely light, Mama Bear woke Patrick, dressed him in a new pair of overalls, and brushed his fur till it shone. She put on her best dress and her favorite hat, then after a quick breakfast, they set off across Ha'Penny Field to the schoolhouse.

It was a yellow-plastered building with a red door and a bell tower, nestled amongst the trees at the end of a playground. Over the door were the words: PECKIN-PAWS' DAY SCHOOL, and from one of the open windows Patrick could hear children singing.

Mama Bear and Patrick entered a dim corridor with a door on either side. They went to the one that said: PRINCIPAL'S OFFICE, and Mama Bear knocked upon it briskly.

"Yes? Who is it?" someone called in an exasperated voice.

Opening the door, Mama Bear and Patrick encountered a stout, old lady rat, sitting behind a broad desk with her paws folded. The old rat peered over her eyeglasses at them and cleared her throat. After Mama

Bear introduced herself, she explained about Patrick. "I want him to be well cared for."

"I see," said the rat with a false smile. "I am Miss Crickaback Peckinpaw. I run the school with my sister, Pickaback, and we try to maintain a Conscientious Curriculum."

"Pardon me?" said Mama Bear.

Miss Peckinpaw, ignoring her, said, "So this is Patrick, is it? Well, young fellow, just go across the hall to room number five and we'll get you started with lessons."

"Thank you," said Mama Bear.

"Thank *you!*" answered Miss Peckinpaw.

Mama Bear took Patrick out in the hall, bent down, and kissed him on both cheeks. "Now, you be a good bear and do what you're told. I will see you this evening," she said.

"Can't you stay a little while?" begged Patrick.

"I have to go to work. Don't worry, you'll have a good time. And when you come home you can tell me all about it." And patting him on the head, Mama Bear rose and slipped out the front door. Patrick hesitated. He did not want to enter that room. He was thinking of hiding somewhere, when he heard noises coming from the principal's office, so he quickly opened the door of room number five.

Inside stood an old rat almost identical to the first,

except that *this* one held a long stick in her paw with
which she was pointing to some letters on a blackboard.
"Who are you?" she demanded, annoyed at being interrupted.

"P-P-Patrick," he stammered.

"What's that? Speak up! One must learn to Enunci-
ate Clearly."

"PATRICK!" he repeated loudly.

"I'll have no shouting in this classroom either, young
fellow. Now, go sit over there. We're in the middle of
a lesson."

To the right of the door were rows of seats arranged
like steps where about a dozen children were seated.

They all looked curiously at Patrick as he climbed up to the top row and sat against the wall, trying not to be noticed.

Patrick thought the morning would never end. Miss Peckinpaw taught vowels from a book called *Professor Ratser's Rhetoric* and called upon several of the children to recite; but to Patrick's relief, most of the time she paid no attention to him.

At noontime, all the children were given graham crackers and milk and allowed to go outside on the playground. But none of the other children asked Patrick to join in their games, so he had to stand apart watching them. "I wish I was home," he said. "This is no fun at all!"

Wandering off among the trees, he sat down on a stone, out of sight of the schoolhouse. "I'll tell Ma I'm not learning *anything*, then she won't make me come to this stupid place anymore!" When he could no longer hear the cries of the children, he decided recess must be over. But when he went back, all the children had already gone inside!

Patrick dashed over to the schoolhouse and into the corridor. He was so upset that he went through the wrong door and wound up in the Principal's office.

Miss Crickaback Peckinpaw was seated at her desk eating cheese and sipping tea from a flowered china cup. "Good Heavens!" she exclaimed. "You almost scared the heart out of me! What's the idea, bursting in here like this?"

"I'm sorry," said Patrick, "I thought . . ."

Miss Peckinpaw rose to her feet. "Well, you come right here. I'll teach you not to burst into a room like a wild animal!" And laying hold of Patrick, she smacked him roughly on the seat of his pants with a ruler. "Now get back to the classroom!"

Angry and humiliated, Patrick returned to room number five. "You're late!" declared the other Miss Peckinpaw. A few of the children started to giggle.

"One must Practice Punctuality," said Miss Peckinpaw. "As an example you are to stand in the corner for the rest of the afternoon."

"No," said Patrick. "I won't!"

"You do what I say, or your mother will hear of this!"

Patrick glared at her for a second, then marched angrily over to the corner muttering, "Your mother will hear of this. . . . Punish me for nothing!" He knew all the other children must be watching him and thinking how stupid he was. And that horrid old Miss Peckinpaw kept striding back and forth, acting as though he wasn't even there. "She's not going to make *me* cry!" Patrick vowed.

When school was over, Patrick raced home. But the house was empty. His mama wasn't there. "Oh, darn!

I forgot; she's at work," thought Patrick. "I'll have to go find her."

He hurried down the hill to Main Street, but when he came to the bottom he stopped short. He had forgotten the name of the bakery shop where Mama Bear was working. Spying a bakery across the street, Patrick ran over, went inside, and asked, "Does my ma work here?" But the salespeople didn't know what he was talking about. So he just ran up and down the blocks, glancing hastily into windows. Nowhere could he find anyone who even *looked* like Mama Bear.

Finally, he trudged miserably up the hill and sat for a long while in the empty house. As the daylight grew dimmer, Patrick became more and more upset. "She's never here when I need her!" he sobbed. "Oh, she doesn't care about me anymore. I'll show her! I'm going to hide in the forest and Ma will think I'm lost, and she'll cry and *cry* . . . and when I come home she'll be so glad to see me she'll never leave me alone again!"

Dashing out the back door, Patrick ran across the yard into the trees. Much of the forest was in shadow, but he followed the patches of sunlight, slipping now and then on twigs or leaves. "This ground *moves* too much!" he fussed. "I didn't know it was going to be so dark in here." It was quiet, too, except for some birds calling high above. As he went, the trees grew closer together and branches scraped his fur. "I guess this is far enough," Patrick thought. He crouched down, sure his mama would never be able to find him, and waited.

It grew darker. Patrick heard queer sounds coming from behind, and felt a wiggling next to his paw. Something flew very close by with a heavy flapping noise, and Patrick, giving a cry, jumped up. "This place is scary. I've stayed in here long enough."

He headed for home, but the house wasn't where it was supposed to be, so he tried a different direction—and slipped down into a gully. "Ma, help!" he wailed, scrambling out. He ran on until he collided with a tree.

Patrick squeezed down tightly between the roots, trembling with the cold, fearful of what might be lurking nearby. Then he remembered Mama Bear's stories. He squinted into the darkness, imagining he could see the red streak of the father fox's brush, or the fat form of the badger loping along. And he began to feel less frightened.

All at once, Patrick saw a light glowing amongst the trees, like a small, orange sun suspended in midair. He got to his feet, rubbed his eyes, and looked again. The light, although some distance away, was moving toward him, illuminating each section of forest it passed. It came from a lantern on a pole carried by a large bear with blue fur and deep, red eyes who wore a lavender gown and a pointed cap that had a star on its tip.

The bear stopped several yards away. Patrick was too

amazed to move—and the bear just looked at him and
didn't move either. In silence they stood and stared at
one another. Then the bear's fur rippled; his nose
twitched in a friendly way; he smiled and extended a
paw.

Running up to him, Patrick sobbed, "I'm lost!"

The bear bent down and gently lifted Patrick up with one arm so that they were face to face. For some reason Patrick was not at all frightened; there was a world of warmth in the bear's red eyes, a comfort in that blue fur. And the longer Patrick looked into the bear's eyes, the more he began to see himself staring back. Smiling again, the bear seemed to say, "I'll take you home. . . . Don't worry, everything will be all right."

Patrick crawled on the bear's shoulder, rested his head against his ears, and the two of them set off together through the dark forest.

Mama Bear was frantic when she came home from work and found Patrick missing. She searched the house from top to bottom, went all the way to the end of Trumble Street calling his name, and was leaving to fetch the police, when she heard a thump at the back door. Pulling it open, she saw Patrick sitting on the step. "Ma!" he cried. ". . . Uh, hullo!"

As she scooped him in her arms, Mama Bear glimpsed a small, orange light hovering amid the trees; then it blinked out, like a candle being snuffed.

She gave Patrick a hot bath and put him to bed before asking what had happened. "Oh, Ma, school was terrible, and those mean teachers punished me for nothing! I never want to go back there. And when I came home, you weren't here, so I ran into the forest.

I didn't mean to, but you made me mad! I got lost, and it was all dark and scary; then this bear with blue fur came and brought me home."

"Bear with blue fur?" said Mama Bear.

"I bet it was the Sandman."

Mama Bear reflected for a moment, then a peaceful smile spread over her face. "No, that wasn't the Sandman. . . . I think it must have been the Lantern Keeper. Grandma often told me about him. She said he's a spirit of the forest who watches over and protects all the animals. I never believed he actually existed, but I'm glad he does, or I mightn't have got you back. I hope I won't have to worry about you every time I go to work."

"I don't *want* you to work!" Patrick replied. "I just want us to do things together."

Mama Bear sighed. "Very well, I'll quit my job, if that's what you want."

"Oh, boy!" shouted Patrick.

"But I'm afraid we won't be able to afford any more fruit to bake pies with, or vegetables for stew. . . . I expect we shall have to live on cereal. No more balloons—too extravagant! And certainly no more toys. . . ."

"No toys?" Patrick cried incredulously. "That's terrible!" He considered, then said, "I guess you'll have to work after all . . . darn!"

"But you can help me, Patrick, by going to school

and learning to do some things by yourself. It's part of growing up."

"I see, Ma," said Patrick. "It was stupid to run away. I'll help you as much as I can, as long as you still love me."

"How silly," Mama Bear said, folding him in her arms. "I'll *always* love you."

After that, Patrick went to school without complaint, although he still didn't like the Peckinpaws! When school was over, he'd come home, fix himself a snack, then play in the yard until evening. As the sun began to set, Patrick walked to the corner of the block where the trolley line ended and sat on a stone wall to wait for Mama Bear. He'd bring some comic books to read under the streetlamp.

At the bottom of the hill he could see the trolley car and hear the faint *ding! ding!* of its bell. The lights of Main Street twinkled in the gathering dusk as people wandered to and fro, shopping or pausing to chat with their neighbors. The rooftops were orange from the falling sun, their chimneys trailing smoke into the sky. It seemed to Patrick that the whole world was spread before him.

Each time the trolley car came rumbling up the hill, Patrick would say to himself, "She's going to be on this one." And if she wasn't, he would go back to reading

his comic book until the next trolley came. And eventually the car with Mama Bear would arrive. She usually looked tired, but her face always brightened at the sight of Patrick.

"Did you bring me anything, Ma?"

"Well, now let me see. . . . What do you suppose I could have brought you?"

"A toy?" asked Patrick. "A coloring book? A puzzle?"

And, still guessing, Patrick would slip his paw

through Mama Bear's arm as they walked off to their little home on the hill.

In the evenings after dinner, Patrick sat on the step by the back door, peering into the forest. He wondered where the Lantern Keeper was, and if he'd ever see him again. There was something both real and unreal about him, like the way Patrick felt when he woke from a dream. He tried to figure it out, but after a time his thoughts always became confused, and he had to think about something else.

Now and then, a fox on its nightly prowl would slip out through the trees near the edge of the wood and stop stiff, listening to secret voices. If the fox did not notice him right away, Patrick would sit still, hardly breathing, to see how far it might come. As the fox drew nearer, he saw its fur glistening in the moonlight and admired the cunning look in its wild, black eyes. He thought he was smarter than the fox to fool it into coming so far. But if it refused to move closer to the house, Patrick would go *"BOO!"* and the fox would start, look in his direction, then dash fearfully into the trees—a blur of red fur. And laughing, Patrick would go happily to bed.

Buddies

ONE OF PATRICK'S favorite things was sliding down the hallway banister, even though Mama Bear had repeatedly told him not to. He usually waited until she was in another room so she never caught him.

But one day he slid off too quickly, tumbled onto the floor, and rolled against a table. Next thing he heard was a crash, and Mama Bear came in from the parlor. "Patrick!" she cried. "That was my grandmother's best vase!"

Looking behind him, Patrick saw a pile of shattered glass. "Oh, sorry," he said. "Well, I have to be going now. . . . 'Bye!"

"Oh no you don't!" She grabbed him by his suspenders. "How many times have I told you *not* to slide down that banister? Now get to your room!"

Afraid she was going to hit him, Patrick ran up the stairs. But when he reached the top, he turned round and said defiantly, "It was an *accident!*"

"And stay there!" cried Mama Bear. Shaking her head, she went into the kitchen for a broom to sweep up the mess.

Patrick stomped angrily into his room and slammed the door. From the open window came a beam of sun. In the distance he could hear someone hammering nails, and the voices of children. "Darn!" he said, climbing out on the roof. "It's too nice a day to be indoors. If Ma stays in the front of the house, and if she doesn't look out the windows, maybe I can play in the back without her seeing me." He went over to the edge of the roof, and carefully descended a trellis to the yard.

Of course he would have to do something quiet— like what? Looking for unusual-shaped rocks? "Yes," he thought. "I'll collect some to use with my slingshot."

He got down on his knees and began rummaging through the tall grass. Suddenly something hard hit him on the nose. "Ow!" Patrick cried. Looking up, he saw a plump bear with tan-colored fur sitting in a crook of the large tree which separated his yard from the next. The bear had a pile of nuts next to him, and held one firmly in his raised paw. "Get away from here!" the bear called rudely. "This is my territory!"

"What do you mean, your territory? This is *my* yard!" said Patrick.

"Not anymore," answered the bear. "I've just made myself king of this spot. From the tree to that rock over there. And you can't play here without my permission." He let go with another nut which struck Patrick's ear.

"Quit that!"

"Make me!"

When Patrick looked more closely, he realized that the bear was bigger than he was, and the tree very high, so it seemed unwise to start a fight. "Well . . . do I have your permission?" he finally asked.

The plump bear considered, as if it was an important decision, then replied, "Only if you swear you aren't an enemy."

"I swear," said Patrick.

"All right, I believe you. Want to come up to my fort?"

"Oh, boy!" Patrick went over to the tree and tried to climb it, but his foot kept slipping on the bark, and there were few places for his paws to grip. Whenever he got up a few inches, he'd just slide to the bottom again.

The other bear, clicking his tongue, said, "What a

little baby! Here, grab hold of my paw." Patrick did, and the bear hoisted him up, then scooted over to give Patrick room to sit. "Hullo. My name is Ted. Let's be buddies!"

"Hullo. I'm Patrick. . . . O.K. You're new around here, aren't you?"

"Yes," answered Ted, "we moved to Puttyville yesterday." They sat on the branch for a while, dangling their legs. "You know," Ted said, "this fort would be even better if it had a barricade."

"What's that?"

"Something you hide behind when enemies are approaching."

"Hmmmmm, my ma has some old wood in the cellar," Patrick suggested. "Maybe we could use that."

"Good idea!" Ted exclaimed, sliding nimbly down from the tree. Patrick followed slowly, and by the time he reached the ground, Ted was already at the house.

"Shh!" Patrick whispered, running up. "My ma doesn't know I'm out here."

They crouched down and slunk round the side of the building. Peeking through one of the kitchen windows, they could see into the hall where Mama Bear stood before a mirror putting on her hat and coat. She went to the head of the stairs and called, "Patrick, I'm going to the grocery. I want you to stay up there until I get back." Then she went out the front door.

"What luck!" Patrick said. "Come on."

He had to stand on a wooden crate in order to reach the latch of the cellar door, but it slid back without difficulty, and he and Ted went down some steps into the darkness. Neither of them was tall enough to reach the light switch; however, a beam of sun from a high window revealed a number of long planks piled against a mound of dirt.

"These boards are too heavy," said Ted as he grabbed one. "We'll never be able to lift them."

Patrick screwed up his eyes and scanned the room. He discovered a good deal of smaller pieces lying about, so they carried these out one by one to the tree.

Ted, climbing back onto the branch, took charge of things, while Patrick handed the wood up to him. He wanted to do all the work himself and wouldn't let Patrick help one bit! He jammed the boards between the boughs, one on top of another. When the barricade was finished, Patrick found that it was deep enough to hide behind and there was a hole in the tree for storing ammunition.

"We need some nuts and twigs and stuff," Ted explained. "Why don't you go down and look for some?"

"Why don't *we* go down and look for some?" Patrick replied.

"But I'm the *General.* Generals aren't supposed to do those things. . . . All right, maybe just this once."

"I thought you said you were the king?"

"Same thing," said Ted.

Soon the hole was well stocked with weapons and useful things. Patrick had gone back to his room for his slingshot; Ted contributed some cookies and a pair of binoculars. They sat there, secure in their fort, looking thoughtfully over the rooftops.

"This is dull," Ted remarked. "Aren't there any enemies about?"

Patrick put his paw to his nose. "There's Big Bear. I guess he's an enemy. He's always trying to beat me up."

"Swell!" cried Ted. "Let's go spy on him. Where's his hideout?"

"I don't know where he lives, but he's almost always over at Ha'Penny Field."

Now Patrick was a little nervous about bothering Big Bear, but he didn't want to seem a spoilsport; besides, he felt bolder with Ted along. Taking the binoculars, they scampered across the yard, out to Trumble Street, where Patrick paused to check if Mama Bear was coming, then down to the end of the block. A quick hop over a small stream led to the field—and sure enough, seated next to his mud puddle was Big Bear.

He was wearing an old yellowed T-shirt, several sizes too small, which was ripped and covered with stains, and patches of his fur were stuck together.

Ted pulled Patrick down beside him in the tall grass, and they lay silently for several seconds. Craning his neck, Ted gave a look through the binoculars. "You're

right," he said. "An enemy if I ever saw one. . . . Take a peek!"

But when Patrick raised the lenses to his eyes, Big Bear had got awfully tiny!

"You're looking through the wrong end!" sighed Ted peevishly.

Patrick, looking again, could see Big Bear scooping up piles of mud with a spoon, which he packed tightly into a metal pail. He would turn the pail upside down, tap the bottom with his paw, and slowly lift it; but it wasn't working very well. The mud just oozed out and collapsed in a lump, causing Big Bear to growl and throw his spoon on the ground.

When this happened four times in a row, Patrick burst out, "Ha, ha, ha, ha! You dumbbell! You can't even make mud pies!"

"Hey!" called Big Bear. "What are you doing?"

"None of your business!" Ted yelled back.

"Oh yeah?" said Big Bear, getting clumsily to his feet. "Don't you make fun of me, you little punks!"

"Run!" shouted Ted. They tore out of the field toward Trumble Street while Big Bear, growling and shaking his fists, came right behind. Patrick and Ted, much faster because they were small, got rather far ahead and nimbly hopped over the stream, but Big Bear slipped and fell into the water with a loud splash.

By the time he crawled out and reached the back-

yard, Patrick and Ted were already ensconced in their fort.

"I see you!" said Big Bear, hopping wildly. "You can't fool me!"

Big Bear tried to climb after them, but he was too heavy. Meanwhile, Ted and Patrick began pelting him with nuts and sticks. Enraged, Big Bear grabbed a low-hanging branch which he yanked up and down, making the other branches sway.

"Look out!" screamed Ted, as part of the barricade became dislodged and sank to the ground. Another board slid loose, then their pile of ammunition spilled.

"What in the world is going on?" Mama Bear was standing at the gate, her arms laden with bundles.

As Big Bear let go of the branch, it snapped back. The tree trembled. Patrick and Ted lost their balance and toppled into the yard. And Big Bear bolted off.

"What is the meaning of this?" Mama Bear demanded. "I told you to stay in your room!"

"Well, um . . ." Patrick said sheepishly. "This is my new buddy, Ted."

Ted, who had got to his feet and was dusting off his fur, said, "Oh, hullo. . . . I think I hear my ma calling me. See you around." Before Mama Bear could say anything, he skedaddled off to his house and slammed the door.

First, Mama Bear made Patrick return all the wood to the cellar, then she sent him back to his room. "Never lets me have any fun!" he grumbled, trudging upstairs, but to himself he thought how nice it felt to have a buddy.

The next morning as Patrick was preparing for school, the doorbell rang, and when he opened it, he found Ted standing on the stoop. "Hullo," said Ted. "Want to walk to school together?"

"Sure," replied Patrick, hurrying inside for his jacket. "I'm leaving now, Ma!"

Mama Bear poked her head out of the kitchen. "I've

never seen you so eager to go to school. Well, have a nice day."

"I will. . . . 'Bye!" He slammed the door and followed after Ted.

As they walked down Trumble Street, Patrick explained, "School is pretty good. You get to do some fun things like playing in the playground and making art projects, but we have to do lessons, which are dull, and sometimes—"

"You don't have to tell *me*," Ted interrupted. "I've been to school before. I'm used to it."

"Oh," said Patrick. He wanted to tell Ted something that would be useful on his first day, but he couldn't think of much. Suddenly he got an inspiration. "Well, I'd better let you know about Miss Peckinpaw. She can be quite horrid, but—"

"Oh, I can handle teachers," said Ted, interrupting again. "Just watch me!"

"Oh," Patrick answered, going very pale. He didn't say anything more until they arrived at the schoolhouse.

The very first thing, Miss Peckinpaw brought Ted up to the front of the class and made a big show of introducing him as the "new pupil." Ted beamed proudly, and Patrick thought that Ted *could* handle teachers.

Ted sat next to Patrick. They kept giggling and nudging each other whenever Miss Peckinpaw's back was turned. And several of the children began giggling, too. Miss Peckinpaw slid her glasses down to the end of her nose, peeked over them, and snorted. After lunch she separated Patrick and Ted.

Handing round crayons and large sheets of manila paper, Miss Peckinpaw requested each pupil to draw a picture of his or her house. "Now, no dragons, or anything nonsensical," she ordered. "I want this to be a realistic depiction of your home . . . understand?"

"Yes, Miss Peckinpaw," chorused the class as they set to work with their crayons.

Patrick, digging round in the crayon box, was trying to find some which weren't broken, when he happened to glance at Ted. Ted was sitting bolt upright, looking confusedly about the classroom. He swallowed a couple of times, held a crayon awkwardly in his paw, and intently put it to the paper.

For a while the only sounds were the children shuffling in their seats and the steady *clop clop* of Miss Peckinpaw's hard shoes moving up and down the rows, pausing now and then to inspect someone's drawing. Patrick finished his picture quickly, but Ted, breathing heavily, had his nose down so far it practically touched the desk. He kept sighing, and the paper kept sticking to his paw.

Finally, Miss Peckinpaw said, "All right, please sign your drawings and pass them to the end of the row. Patrick, you collect them for me."

Patrick hopped out of his seat and swiftly gathered all the papers. He couldn't understand why Ted looked so troubled.

After he had returned to his seat, Miss Peckinpaw went to her lectern and studied the pictures, singling one out now and then and making comments. When she came to Patrick's, she exclaimed, "Now this is lovely!" She held it in front of her so the class could see. "Very good, Patrick."

Patrick squirmed happily in his seat as Miss Peckinpaw pinned his drawing to the bulletin board. Returning to the lectern, she continued going through the pictures—then her pinched old face contorted into a sour grimace, and she cried, "Who did *this*?"

There was no response from the class.

"Well?" said Miss Peckinpaw.

". . . 's mine," Ted answered in a small voice.

"Well, you should be ashamed of yourself! I said 'drawing'—not *scribbling*!" And she flung the paper angrily at Ted. "You're going to have to learn not to fool around if you intend to remain in my classroom."

Ted, embarrassed, picked up his picture.

When the children poured into the playground after school, Patrick found Ted and walked beside him. He held his drawing proudly in his paws, giving it another look. "I can't wait till Ma sees this," he said. "Maybe she'll let me put it up in the kitchen."

Ted, who had spoken not a word, said all at once, "Oh, you think you're so big, just because you can draw stupid old pictures! Drawing is sissy stuff anyway!" With that, he gave Patrick a hard shove, causing him to let go of the drawing. It fluttered onto the grass, but when Patrick ran to clutch it, the strong winds pushed it farther away. No matter how quickly Patrick raced after the drawing, just as he got close, it was blown out

of his reach, until a large gust lifted it over his head, carrying it up to the tree branches.

Patrick could hear Ted and some of the other children laughing at him. "It's gone!" he sobbed. "Now I can't show it to Ma!" And with his paw over his face, he ran off crying.

Mama Bear found him lying on his bed when she got home. Tears still glistened in the corners of his eyes.

"Patrick, what's the matter?"

"Oh . . . nothing, Ma. I just lost a drawing I did for you, that's all."

Sitting next to him on the bed, Mama Bear said, "Well, you can make me another one, can't you?"

"I guess so. . . . Ma, I don't think I want any dinner tonight."

Mama Bear put her paw to his forehead. "Are you sick?"

"No . . . I'm just not hungry."

The next morning, Patrick did not feel even slightly better. As Mama Bear ladled farina into his cereal bowl, he sat staring blankly at the tablecloth and wouldn't say anything. Mama Bear put her paw on her hip, and with her other paw tapped the empty farina spoon against her apron. "Patrick, are you sure you're feeling all right?"

"No, Ma," he said. "I'm not feeling good at all. I

don't think I'd better go to school today."

So Mama Bear took him upstairs, stuck a thermometer in his mouth, went into the bathroom and brought out a bottle of tummy medicine. The last thing Patrick wanted to do was drink the thick, bluish liquid in that bottle, but it was easier than facing Ted and the other children. After she had removed the thermometer and held it up to the light, Mama Bear poured two heaping tablespoonfuls of medicine and gave them to Patrick.

"You don't have a temperature," she said. "Still, I can't leave you alone if you're sick. I'd better stay home today."

"No, Ma, you don't have to. I'll be O.K."

Mama Bear frowned uncertainly. In the end, she went to work, but promised to come home earlier than usual. Patrick, whose tummy had been fine until it had the dreadful medicine poured down it, went to the kitchen as soon as she left and ate two bowls of farina, a glass of milk, and six graham crackers to get rid of the taste. Then he sat on the back stoop, gazing at the big tree, where only the other day he and Ted had had such good times.

It was a slow day. Patrick played with his toys and read his comic books, but he wished he was playing outside in the sun with his friends.

At three o'clock Mama Bear returned home and found Patrick feeling much better. She was in the

kitchen, and Patrick in the parlor, when the doorbell sounded. He went to answer it—but when he opened the door no one was there! Looking down, Patrick saw a familiar piece of paper lying on the stoop. It was his drawing, crumpled and slightly dirty, although someone had gone to a deal of trouble attempting to smooth out the wrinkles. And . . . *and* on the bottom corner in small lettering someone had written, "I'm sorry. Let's be buddies again."

"Ma!" he called. "I'm going next door to visit Ted."

"Well, if you're sure you're feeling better," Mama Bear said.

"Oh, I feel a hundred percent better now!"

Later, Patrick and Ted were sitting on Patrick's roof with their paws round each other. "You know, I've

been thinking," said Ted. "When we build our clubhouse, you can draw pictures for the walls."

"Clubhouse?" said Patrick.

"Sure, I figure we'll build it right there on my side
of the tree. . . . Of course, if we build it in my yard,
that means I'll have to be president."

"Of course," said Patrick.

The Candy Store

PATRICK WOKE up one morning wanting to go someplace. He hopped out of bed, got dressed, and went down to the kitchen where Mama Bear was sorting laundry. "Why don't we go to the park today?" he asked, pouring himself a glass of milk.

"I can't," replied Mama Bear. "I have a lot of housework to do. Maybe you can find something to do with Ted."

"No, he told me yesterday that he's going to go visit relatives," said Patrick.

Mama Bear interrupted her work to take a bowl of strawberries and some wheat germ and apples from the pantry. As they were eating breakfast, she said, "Well, you're big enough now to go downtown by yourself."

"I know, but that's no fun! Maybe I'll go exploring."

Mama Bear mixed her wheat germ in with the strawberries. "That sounds like a good idea—it will keep you out of my way—just don't go near any deep culverts, or too far down the Old Road."

"Sure," said Patrick. He carried his dishes to the sink, then ran up to his room, dug about in the closet, and took out a battered cigar box filled with numerous odds and ends. Down at the bottom were three pennies and a nickel. "I *thought* these were still in here," he said, stuffing the money into his trouser pocket. He also took his slingshot in case he met any ferocious animals.

At first Patrick couldn't decide where to go. There wasn't much left to discover in the park, and he was always hanging about the train station, so he went over to Ha'Penny Field, but even that looked ordinary and unexciting. "How boring!" he thought.

Patrick glanced to where the Old Road ran along the outskirts of the field and disappeared into the trees. He began to feel mischievous. Since Mama Bear had warned him against going there, he thought it would be fun to disobey her. "She'll never know. I always find my way back," he thought smugly.

It was an early autumn morning: The sunlight was brilliant, the trees smelled sharp, and the dirt beneath

68

his feet was as warm as new-baked bread. As he went, Patrick sang to himself in his high scratchy voice:

"My name is Patrick Pahnee
My name is Patrick Pog!
Good old Patrick Pahnee
Good old Patrick Pog!"

He went on, and he went on, and he went on some more—into the heart of the forest. Just when he was growing tired of looking at nothing but trees, he rounded a curve in the road and came out upon a neat little building sitting in the shade of two spreading oaks. A sign was perched above the red roof that said: CANDY STORE and below was a large window where all kinds of colorful and tasty-looking candy was displayed. Hurrying forward, Patrick pressed his nose to the glass. "Oh, boy!" he cried. "A candy store! Just what I've been looking for!"

He went right up to the door and opened it. The proprietor, Mr. Ollie Arwood, wearing a yellow shirt and brass-buckled suspenders, sat behind a glass counter next to the cash register. As the bell over the door sounded, he looked up and said, "Hullo, may I help you?"

Patrick was giving a good look round. There were racks filled to the brim with comic books with cello-

phane covers, magazines, notepads, and packaged toys. Along one wall ran a shelf holding an assortment of miniature cameras with their own carrying cases, and sheets of decals, and bottles filled with fruit juice. "My name is Patrick Pahnee Pog," he answered at last, "but Patrick is my everyday name. Some place you've got here."

". . . Oh, thanks," said Ollie. "Do you want to buy something?"

Stepping closer, Patrick gazed into the counter. He had never seen so much candy in all his life: rows of fudge, peppermint sticks, jawbreakers, wax teeth, licorice twists, and marzipan pigs! He wished he had enough money to buy everything—but then he saw a tray of bright red candy which looked best of all!

"Yes, I'd like some of those little red things."

"Well," Ollie replied, "they're two cents each. How many do you want?"

Patrick thought a moment, then said, "I'll take four."

Ollie reached under the counter, withdrew four of the little red things, and put them in a white paper bag. "That will be eight cents."

Patrick spread his pennies on the counter, took his bag of candy, and went over to the comic-book rack. He glanced at all the covers, then began to spin the rack around. "How much are these?" he asked.

"Ten cents apiece," said Ollie. "But don't spin that rack so fast—and don't mess them up!"

Suddenly, Patrick noticed one with a bright blue cover called "Nuts Boy Funnies" that had a picture of "The Nuts Boy" on the front. He turned to the first page and sat down on the floor to read it.

"Listen, if you're going to buy one, O.K., but I don't allow reading in here."

Glaring at him, Patrick said, "What a grouch!"

"Don't you call *me* names!" cried Ollie, rushing from behind the counter. "Put that book back right now!"

Patrick got up and stuffed the comic book sloppily behind some others, but as he did so, the rack swayed off balance and toppled to the floor, scattering books in all directions.

Ollie cried, "Now look what you've done!"

"Oh, sorry," said Patrick, dashing for the door. "Well, I have to be going now. . . . 'Bye!"

"Come back here. And don't slam that—"

SLAM!!! went the door.

Patrick trotted down the road the way he had come. "Ha! Ha! I'm a lucky bear!" he thought. "I got out of the store without having to pick up the comic books. I sure would like to have that 'Nuts Boy Funnies,' only I don't have ten cents . . . darn! I wonder if Ma will give me a dime if I ask her nicely?"

He became so excited that he ran the rest of the way home. Mama Bear was in the kitchen bent over a washtub with a scrub board, busy doing laundry. Wet clothes were hung from a rack in front of the stove to dry, there were pillowcases, handkerchiefs, and other linens piled on the table, and water was spilled liberally about the floor.

"There you are, Patrick," said Mama Bear, wiping her eyes with the back of her paw. "Would you please take that pail of laundry outside for me?"

"Sure, Ma. . . ." Patrick grabbed one handle of the metal pail, dragged it across the doorway, and down the

stoop to the yard. Setting it under the clothesline, he
hurried back. "Ma, can I have a—"

"Patrick, fill the clothespin bag up," she went on.
"Then go play, and I'll call you when lunch is ready."

"But, Ma, I—"

"Please don't pester me! Can't you see I've got a ton
of work to do?"

"Yes," said Patrick. He threw several pawfuls of
clothespins into the bag and shuffled outdoors. There
was no use bothering Mama Bear when she was in one
of her cranky moods. He went over to the swing and
listlessly rocked to and fro, munching on his candy.

"If I don't get that comic book soon someone else
may buy it. How annoying!"

In a little while the back door opened, and Mama Bear appeared carrying Patrick's lunch on a tray. "Things are such a mess in the kitchen. I thought you would be more comfortable out here."

"Thanks. Oh, by the way, can I have a—"

"I'd join you, but I haven't time," she said as she placed the tray on an upturned basket. Then she bustled back in the house before Patrick could say anything.

Eating his sandwich, Patrick grew more and more impatient. "It's not fair! All I need is a stupid old dime!" Then he thought he'd better go back to the Candy Store after lunch just to see if there was more than one copy. He gulped down his milk, grabbed his cap, and ran out of the yard, not even bothering to take in the tray.

And all the way down the Old Road he kept muttering, "I hope it's not gone. . . . I hope it's not gone!"

He rushed up to the Candy Store and burst in the door. When he saw the "Nuts Boy Funnies" sticking up from the top of the comic-book rack he felt much better.

Ollie, coming out of the back room, said, "Yes, may I help . . . Oh, no! It's that bratty bear again!"

"What?"

". . . Uh, nothing. What do you want *now*?"

"Just looking," said Patrick. "Something wrong with that?"

"Not if you behave yourself!" Ollie, who was unpacking cartons, returned to his work, as Patrick eagerly removed the comic book and held it lovingly in his paws. At that moment, Patrick wanted it more than anything else in the world!

He was looking to see how many copies were left, when Ollie picked up a carton and disappeared into the back room. A sudden idea occurred to Patrick. He hesitated. Then he quickly stuck the comic book under his arm. "I think I'll go now, Mr. Man," he called. Ollie did not reply. And Patrick sped out the door and down the Old Road, the book tucked tightly against his body. It wasn't until he spied the sloping roofs of Puttyville that he slowed to his usual pace. "I *am* a lucky bear," he said. "I got this book without having to pay for it."

He *almost* felt guilty about stealing, but he said, "Oh, it's only a comic book. No one will ever know." And he began singing again in his high scratchy voice:

> *"My name is Patrick Pahnee*
> *My name is Patrick Pog!*
> *Clever old Patrick Pahnee*
> *Clever old Patrick Pog!"*

When he reached home, Mama Bear was out in the yard, pinning sheets to the clothesline. "Where have you been?" she said crossly. "I've been looking all over for you!"

"Look, Ma!" replied Patrick, proudly holding up his comic book.

"Now where did you get that?"

"At this little candy store in the woods. I found a dime on the Old Road and . . ."

"I thought I told you not to go down there!"

"Oh, I didn't go very far . . . honest. Aren't I lucky to have found a whole dime?"

"I suppose," said Mama Bear, "but from now on, do what I tell you." She continued pulling laundry from a basket and putting it up to dry. Patrick, going over to the big tree, thought, "She bought the whole story!" He crawled down in a hollow of the trunk to read his book.

By the time Mama Bear had emptied the last basket, the afternoon was getting windy and the sunlight began to fade. Patrick heard footsteps coming along the side of the house and glanced up to see Ollie Arwood approaching. A shiver shot through him.

Rapidly stuffing the comic book into his back trouser pocket, Patrick ran and hid behind his mama's skirt. "It's Mr. Man from the Candy Store!" he cried. "Don't let him get me! I'm sorry I stole that comic book. . . . Please! I'll never do it again!"

"Stole?" Mama Bear echoed. "Patrick, how could you?!"

Ollie leaned upon the gate and said, "Evening. Are you Mrs. Pog?"

When she nodded, Ollie continued, "Some neighbors told me where to locate you. I believe your son, Patrick, dropped his cap when he was in my store this afternoon."

"Is *that* all!" mumbled Patrick.

After thanking him, Mama Bear brought Patrick out and made him apologize for swiping the book; then she

took a dime from her apron pocket and handed it to Ollie. "Please excuse Patrick," she explained. "He has a *lot* to learn!"

Ollie smiled good-naturedly and wished them a nice evening. As soon as he left, Mama Bear turned to Patrick. "I'm extremely disappointed in you! Not only did you *steal*, you *lied* to me! I want you to go to your room for the rest of the evening!"

Patrick's face dropped. He stumbled upstairs feeling ashamed and not the least bit lucky anymore. Once inside his room, he removed the "Nuts Boy" comic from his trouser pocket and looked at it again, but it no longer seemed special, so he flung it across the room and went to lie down on his bed. He stayed there for a long time, staring at the ceiling, snuffling now and then, or brushing a tear from his eyes while the room grew dark. Below came sounds of Mama Bear working in the kitchen, and Patrick realized that she hadn't called him down to dinner. "She doesn't want to be around me because I'm a *thief!*" he thought. He turned his face to the wall and cried.

Much later, he heard the *thump, thump, thump* of Mama Bear's slippers coming upstairs. "Now I'm going to get spanked!" he decided.

The door opened, letting in light from the hall, and Mama Bear stood there for a moment, her face in shadow. As she entered the room, Patrick noticed she was carrying a tray of food. "I've fixed you some soup," she said coldly, setting the tray on a stool by the bed.

Patrick raised himself to a sitting position. "Thank you, Ma."

She looked down at him, her face still stern. "Patrick, I don't ever want you to do something like that again. Stealing is wrong!"

"I won't, Ma."

Then Mama Bear sat down on the edge of the bed. "Why didn't you simply *ask* me for the money?"

"I tried, only you were too busy."

"Couldn't you have waited until I wasn't busy?"

"But I thought the book would be gone, and I wanted it right away."

"Well, you're going to have to learn to be more patient from now on."

"Are you patient?"

Mama Bear smiled and smoothed the folds of her apron. "I think I'm *very* patient with you. Now would you like some cookies for dessert?"

"Oh, sure!" cried Patrick. But before Mama Bear left to get them, Patrick grasped hold of her paw. "You know, Ma, I guess I'm a lucky bear after all!"

The Rock House

BY THE TIME October rolled around, the forest behind Patrick's house was a multitude of warm colors: gold, orange, yellow, brown. The crisp winds blew the leaves from the tree branches and Mama Bear took a rake from the cellar, with which she gathered the leaves into piles. Patrick scooped them up and dumped them into wooden baskets and the wheelbarrow. The leaves, dry as sand, crumbled unless you handled them carefully. Mama Bear selected a few to keep for decorating the kitchen, while the rest she dumped in a huge heap in the most open spot in the yard.

That night, Ted came over and they made a bonfire.

It was pleasant to sit before the crackling flames, warm in the chill night, to toast marshmallows and watch the fire curl like a great orange genie into the darkness. But Patrick thought there was something uncomfortable about the season, too. The sun never seemed to rise very high, and frequently a gray shadow hung over the land.

One overcast day, Patrick went into the backyard to play. It was cumbersome because of wearing a jacket. He dug a hole in the ground, and when it was deep enough, he buried some toy trains and cars in it. Then he heard a snapping of leaves and saw Ted striding up carrying something in his paws.

"What do you have there?" Patrick inquired.

"A bomb," said Ted proudly.

"A bomb, you stupid!"

"No, it's real!" Ted shouted.

"I don't believe you," said Patrick. Then after a few seconds, he asked, "You mean it'll really work?"

"Yes," answered Ted. "Look, I've even got a fuse on it." The bomb was a small wax ball in which a leftover squib had been concealed with only the fuse still showing.

Patrick leaned forward in fascination, examining it closely. "Where should we explode it?"

Ted thought this over. "Up at the old Rock House, come on!"

Instead of going to the end of Trumble Street which led to Ha'Penny Field, Patrick and Ted went in the opposite direction, across the vacant lot and straight into the forest. Down a curving road, away from all the other houses, the Rock House sat perched upon its summit of stone like some awesome beast of night. It had been there for as long as anyone in Puttyville could remember, always deserted, dark and mysterious. The wind would whistle through its upper floors—dry screams through broken glass—and once Ted claimed he saw a cutoff head floating behind the windows. All the kids were afraid to go near the place and today the Rock House looked even gloomier than ever.

They went up a row of cold stone steps which ran along the side of the house leading to a deep yard of wild unkempt grass. Before they reached the top, Ted cried, "Halt! We'll explode it here!"

He set the bomb carefully upon the last step but one, and they stood in silence, regarding it for several seconds. A shutter banged above them.

"H-how do you work it?" said Patrick nervously.

Ted pondered a moment. "I think . . ."

"Aren't you supposed to light the fuse with a fire?" Patrick asked.

Ted's mama had forbidden him to play with matches, so he said quickly, "No, I believe you're supposed to pull it out." Swallowing hard, he picked up the wax ball and tugged on the fuse. It would not come loose.

"Pull harder," said Patrick. "Hurry! I don't want to be up here much longer!"

Ted gave the fuse one furious yank and it came out. A little trail of black powder trickled onto the step. "Run!" screamed Ted, dropping the bomb. And they ran as fast as they could, down the steps, down the road, and clear over to a good-sized tree. "We'll be safe here," Ted said. "It should go off any minute."

After waiting for ten whole minutes, Patrick looked curiously at Ted. "Oh, darn!" Ted said. "It was a dud!"

From then on, Patrick could not get the Rock House out of his mind. It was the one place Ted, who was always bragging about his accomplishments, had never been. "If I went in there, Ted would think I'm very brave," Patrick decided, but every time he thought about it, a chill raced down his spine to the tip of his tail.

At night, the timber wolves howled in the dark forest, and above the October moon loomed white and full of secrets. The wind began to wail mournfully, throwing twigs and leaves against the door. Patrick and Mama Bear chucked more logs on the fire, warm and secure in their little parlor. And with each passing day, Patrick grew less confident about entering the haunted Rock House.

Then, one foggy day, as Halloween approached, Mama Bear took him downtown to buy a jack-o'-lantern. The greengrocer had only a few skimpy ones left. "Oh, nuts!" said Mama Bear. "I should have thought of it sooner. What is Halloween without a jack-o'-lantern?"

"Why don't you get two little ones and set them on top of each other?" the grocer suggested.

"No, it has to be a big one or nothing," said Mama Bear.

The grocer stroked his chin in a cogitating way, then said, "I hear there's a patch of wild pumpkins growing in the yard of the Rock House, just ripe for picking. You might try there—that is, if you don't mind a haunted pumpkin. Heh, heh!"

"Oh, I'll go get one . . . please, Ma?" Patrick entreated.

"Well, I don't know . . ." said Mama Bear.

"Please, I'll be real careful. . . ."

"I don't suppose we have much choice," she said. "All right, but come directly home."

Patrick ran off, thinking that if he got a pumpkin from the yard of the Rock House, he could brag about it to all the kids, and they would admire his bravery, even Ted! "No one's ever been in the yard before," he thought. When he came in sight of the Rock House, he slowed down. It looked awfully scary, but he *had* to go up there. He hopped up the stone steps out into the yard.

It was a roomy place and seemed to be a depository for old tin cans, broken garden equipment, nuts, leaves, bicycle tires, and other unwanted articles. One side dropped sharply to the road below, while the other rose to a hill of somber trees. The end of the yard was the forest itself—and there, in a mist-shrouded corner, Patrick saw a patch of enormous pumpkins.

Eagerly, he rushed forward, chosing the first one he could find. Employing the lid of a tin can, he severed the pumpkin from its stalk and tucked it under his paw.

All at once, he heard a queer rustling sound.

At the end of the yard a figure was moving toward him through the mist. Patrick started to scream for help, but then a friendly voice said, "Hullo, what are *you* doing up here?"

It was Ted!

"Oh, hullo," said Patrick, utterly disappointed. "I came to fetch a pumpkin for my ma."

"I thought so," Ted went on matter-of-factly. "That's why I followed you. Great spot for pumpkins—free, too. I came and got ours yesterday."

"Oh," said Patrick.

That night he sat at the kitchen table while Mama Bear scooped the seeds from his pumpkin. When it was

hollowed out, she carved a magnificent face on the front, put a lighted candle inside, and placed the pumpkin in the window. But Patrick did not get much pleasure from it. He kept thinking how much braver than he Ted was.

On Halloween night, Patrick and Ted went Trick-or-Treating with their friend Weaver Bear. Patrick was dressed as a ghost, Ted a vampire, and Weaver a devil. After they had tried most of the houses in the neighborhood, Patrick said, "Let's go to Mr. Man's Candy Store."

"Good idea," said Ted. "He's sure to have plenty of treats for us."

The forest was black as cinders, so they tried to remain on the Old Road. Now and then, one of them would veer off to the side and stumble into a hole or a clump of toadstools. Owls hooted and unseen things slithered across the ground, but Patrick, although frightened, could not bear for Ted to think him a coward, so he kept his mouth shut. And after a bit, they spotted the cheery lights of the Candy Store with its jack-o'-lantern in the window.

Ollie Arwood was lining up rows of candy apples when Ted, Patrick, and Weaver Bear entered.

"Trick or treat!" they called in unison, holding open their bags. Into each, Ollie dropped a candy apple along with assorted sweets.

"Thanks," said Patrick. "Wow! You've really got this place fixed up!" They glanced round, admiring the colored leaves Ollie had taped to the counter, the selection of masks and witches' hats, the orange and black candies made in the shape of pumpkins, and especially a group of cardboard skeletons which dangled from the ceiling on threads.

"These are to keep the goblins and witches away," Ollie said, giving the skeletons a twirl.

"Oh, I'm not afraid of spooks!" Patrick scoffed.

"Well, stay away from the Rock House tonight," Ollie warned. "That place is full of them!"

When they were outside again, Weaver said, "What's all this talk about the Rock House?"

"It's *haunted*, don't you know?" Ted replied. "All the kids are afraid to go inside because of the spooks."

"I'm not afraid," said Patrick.

"Hogwash!" Ted laughed. "You're the biggest scare-dy-cat around!"

"I am not! I can go in there anytime I want!" Patrick shouted.

"What about tonight?"

"Well . . . um . . ." Patrick hesitated.

"This I've got to see!" cried Weaver, very excited. "How long will you *stay* in there?"

"Oh, ten minutes," Patrick answered.

Now that he had committed himself, there was no

way for Patrick to back out, so they went down the Winding Way to the Rock House.

In the eerie moonlight, its windows looked like eight eyes peering down at them, and the wind moaned through the rafters. They marched up the steps to the yard. Cobwebs were draped round the edges of the door, just as they adorned the windowsills. It seemed no one had entered in years.

Swallowing hard, Patrick gave his candy bag to Weaver and approached the oak door. "Ten minutes," Ted reminded him.

To Patrick's surprise, the door slid inward rather easily—but with an ominous creaking sound—and he entered a cavernous hallway hung with old lamps long past usefulness. Pastoral prints hung crookedly along the right wall against yellow peeling paper that had once displayed a pattern of roses. There were carpets over the musty floor, but they were so torn in spots that he could see a good portion of the cracked wood beneath. Along the hallway, doors led to dark empty rooms. Patrick stood cowering in the middle of the entrance and thought, "I hope the spooks don't get me!"

Outside, Ted had begun to frown and fidgit. "If Patrick stays in there, everyone will think he's braver than me. Wait here!" he told Weaver. He ran over to

the side of the building, carefully raised a window, and crawled inside.

"This is getting ridiculous!" Weaver said to himself.

Patrick, leaning against a wall, took a deep breath and wondered if his ten minutes were up. All at once, from another room came a hollow moan which reverberated through the house. "Yeow!" Patrick screamed. He dashed for the door, but in the darkness could not find the doorknob. The moan rose again, louder than before. "Help!" cried Patrick. Finally, he located the knob, yanked the door open, and sped into the yard.

When Ted saw him leave, he started to laugh. "Ho! That Patrick sure is a coward!"

Suddenly, another moan came piercingly from the foot of the stairs. "Yeow!" screamed Ted. He charged out the door and slammed into Patrick. "Let's get out of here!" he cried.

"Wait!" Patrick screeched. "Where's Weaver?"

"He's gone!" said Ted. "The spooks must have eaten him!"

They were ready to escape down the steps when Weaver came strolling casually out the front door. "You're right." He laughed. "I guess this place *is* haunted!"

"You tricked me!" cried Ted.

"Isn't that what Halloween is for?" said Weaver.

But Patrick, rolling on the ground, was holding his sides and giggling no end—it turned out Ted wasn't so brave after all!

Secrets

ONE RAINY SATURDAY in November, Patrick was lying in front of the parlor fireplace skimming through *Gilbert's Christmas Catalog.* Gilbert's, though small, was Puttyville's only department store, the full title being "Gilbert's Variety & Toy Emporium," and every year it issued a catalog chock-full of gifts, novelties, and toys. This was the first winter Patrick and Mama Bear would be spending in Puttyville, and since his birthday was only a couple of weeks before Christmas, it would be a double treat!

There were so many things in the catalog to choose from that Patrick was having difficulty deciding what to ask for. Top choice was between a shiny pushcart, painted mauve, and a wooden wagon with *RACER* marked in black letters on its side.

Just then, Mama Bear called him from the kitchen. Owing to the gloomy weather, she had decided to bake a pie so they could have a cozy tea. There were numerous varieties in her red-covered recipe book: Nutmeg pies, Pecan pies, Rhubarb, and Lemon Meringue, but Patrick and Mama Bear thought Peach sounded the most appetizing—a peach pie with orange rind mixed in it.

"Oh, nuts!" said Mama Bear. "I'm plumb out of oranges!"

"Do we have to have orange rind?" Patrick asked.

"No . . . only that's what made it so intriguing," Mama Bear mused. Then she said, "Unless you'd like to go buy some for me?"

Patrick's eyes brightened: If he went downtown, he'd be able to take a peek in Gilbert's and see the wagon and the pushcart close up. So he dashed upstairs for his raincoat. Mama Bear gave him her umbrella, a list for "3 med. size oranges; 1 stick of cinnamon; 1 small tin of ground cloves," and some money.

Outside everything was gray: the hills, the houses on them, the trees, the fences, and the clouds, which were the grayest of all. The only sound was the even buzz of falling rain, splattering on the ground and forming rivulets in the moist dirt. Patrick set off briskly, avoiding puddles.

There were fewer people on Main Street than usual. Gilbert's was dark, humid, and quiet, with the toys sitting silently on shelves the only bright spots. Helga Barns, the saleslady, nodded to Patrick in a familiar way, but kept an eye on him. Patrick went slowly down every row, examining all the merchandise, until he came to an open spot near the back where the larger toys were displayed. Sure enough, there sat the wagon and the pushcart! Patrick climbed into each, imagining he was driving down a very steep hill. Suddenly, Helga Barns came over. Patrick thought he was going to be yelled at, but instead, Helga said, "Patrick, would you do me a favor?"

"What kind of favor?"

"Well, Old Wolfgang the Balloon Man ordered two packages of nails and screws yesterday, and I'm afraid with all this rain he's forgotten to come pick them up. . . . I was wondering if you'd deliver them for me?"

"Sure!" Patrick cried, curious to see what Old Wolfgang's home looked like. "I'm good at errands. I'm on an errand for my ma right now." He climbed carefully off the pushcart and said, "I guess these toys are real expensive, huh?"

"Oh, not terribly," said Helga Barns. "Now, here is Old Wolfgang's address. It's that narrow alleyway at the end of Main Street."

"Oh, I can find it," Patrick replied as he took the bag of nails and screws. "You can count on me." When he headed out of the store the rain had let up.

Old Wolfgang lived in a tall crooked house on a corner, with a sloping roof, peeling plaster, and a yard enclosed by a high wooden fence.

Patrick rang the bell several times, but there was no answer; then he knocked extra loudly—and still nothing. So he tried the door, which was unlocked, and went in. The house, in a shocking state of disarray, was dim and musty, so cluttered that Patrick had to maneuver past cartons, furniture, and circus ornaments to avoid knocking things over. "What fascinating stuff!" he thought. "I wonder where Old Wolfgang got it from?"

Hearing a clanking noise out back, Patrick went through the kitchen—piled with dirty dishes, empty cereal boxes, milk bottles, and paper sacks—to the yard.

In the middle of the yard stood a wondrous little carousel! It had a gold ball perched atop a canopy of red and green stripes with a scalloped edge patterned with stars. A group of stiff but incredibly lifelike animals were poised at the gallop as if waiting to take off:

a pony, a giraffe, two sheep, a lion, and a goat. They circled a cylindrical column ornamented with mirrors and gold leaf. Old Wolfgang was half hidden under the round wood base, with only his legs sticking out, hammering at something, but when he heard Patrick open the kitchen door, he quickly scooted out. "What? What? Woola, woola! Who is trespassing on my property?"

"It's me . . . Patrick Pog."

Old Wolfgang, hopping to his feet, ran forward waving his arms in front of him. "You haven't seen *anything*!" he shouted. "Into the house—go!"

When Patrick had retreated to the kitchen, Old Wolfgang came in after him, shut the door, and frowned. His cheeks were very pink. He had little blue dot eyes and wispy white hair growing all over his head and the bottom of his face. "You are a bad bear to spy on an old man!"

"I wasn't spying!" said Patrick. "Helga Barns at the Variety Store asked me to deliver your screws."

"My what? Screws? Oh, woola, woola! How confusing! No wonder I was having difficulties." He snatched the bag from Patrick and stuck his nose inside. "Yes, these are them; what I ordered. How did *you* get them?"

Patrick sighed and said, "I told you, Miss Barns—"

"No matter . . . I am discovered!" Old Wolfgang went on. He slumped into a chair, sitting on a tin of tea, and opened a box of cookies. Taking one for himself, he handed one to Patrick. "But no publicity. Not yet. Because it is broken . . . rusted . . . it may never run anymore. And such a beautiful little carousel it was!"

Patrick shuffled about, trying to sneak another look at the carousel through the kitchen window. "It's wonderful!" he said. "It would be perfect for the park."

Old Wolfgang chuckled. "Hoo, hoo! So you have guessed my plan. You are a clever bear." He stuffed a few more cookies into his mouth and said, "It is good to eat, rest my old bones. Always I am working on the little carousel, except when I go to sell balloons. It is my dream to have a ride for all the children, or many rides—an amusement park, who knows?"

"Did you build it?" asked Patrick, helping himself to a cookie.

"No, I bought it long ago when I was just starting out, from a marvelous toy maker and mechanical wizard. That's how I began my career. Originally it was atop a wagon. I used to wheel it round the countryside, and whenever I came to a town, all the children would trail after it like streamers. I charged a penny a ride . . . hoo, hoo! Very cheap, but it supported me well enough, my little carousel. What a beautiful sight, with its tinkly melodies and its bright paint! It spun like a top, and laughter from the children came singing out of it. Lovely songs it played—all the old gay tunes one never hears anymore. Waltzes mostly. 'The Clocks.' 'The Trinket Fair.' And 'Lavender Rose.' I did magic tricks and sold balloons.

"As time went on, I hired performers to travel with me: There was Rubicund Rind, the fire-eating pig; Crackbaggy the witch; and Wittychap the clown. We called ourselves 'The Canary Company.' Over the years the troupe split up, with everyone going separate ways. And by the time I came to Puttyville, the carousel was tired and run-down, so all I could do was sell balloons. But—ah!—the days of giving pageants in the provinces! I have those afternoons preserved like a postcard in my brain! By now, all the children have probably grown up and forgotten the music of the little carousel. I guess it is only the old like me who still have a part of us in yesterday."

Waking from his reverie, Old Wolfgang glanced out the window. "Woola! It is raining again! Quick, I must cover my carousel before it rusts!" He burst into the yard, and Patrick followed. They flung canvas sheets over the carousel, fastening them by ropes tied to stakes in the ground, just like a circus tent, and not until it was well protected did they return to the house. "You see how it is," Old Wolfgang explained, "even the weather is against me. Soon it will be winter—no good working in the snow—oh, if only I were a *young* old man!"

Leading Patrick through the room of circus ornaments, he said, "You are a nice, concerned bear. We shall be friends, but you must help keep my secret. People might think I am just an old fool with crazy dreams if they found out. Until I can get the carousel going, nobody must know!"

"Oh, you can count on me," said Patrick.

Old Wolfgang smiled and ruffled the fur on Patrick's head.

Patrick was so excited after he left Old Wolfgang that he was nearly up the hill before he remembered his errand for Mama Bear. He had to go all the way back to the greengrocer's and arrived home very close to teatime.

"Patrick!" said Mama Bear. "Where on earth have you been?"

"Getting your stuff!"

"But it shouldn't have taken you *this* long." She tapped her foot. "What were you up to anyway?"

"I can't tell," said Patrick. "It's a secret."

That night, Patrick lay in bed listening to the sound of raindrops falling into an empty tin can in the garden. There was something comforting about the hollow *plunk plunk* as the can filled with water, and a soothing feeling spread over Patrick's body. It had to do with birthdays and pushcarts and a secret no one but he and Old Wolfgang knew about.

The rain turned to snow during the night, falling without a sound, and in the morning there were drops of ice hanging from the roof. "This is pleasant!" thought Patrick, looking into the backyard. He rushed through breakfast, then, bundling up with a scarf and mittens, scurried outside and dug trenches in the snow.

Ted came over and they tossed snowballs back and forth until Mama Bear made them come in for lunch.

After lunch, Patrick and Ted went into the forest with the wheelbarrow to hunt for pinecones. How silent everything was! No birdsong, nor movement of animals—just the unending white carpet that crunched under their feet, leaving little pits behind them.

They came across dozens of pinecones lying in a heap beneath a tall fir tree. Something had knocked them all down—the wind? An animal? What?

"Something *secret*," Ted said as they loaded the pinecones into the wheelbarrow.

"*I* have a secret," Patrick replied, then wished he hadn't.

"Oh, what is it?"

"I can't tell—because it's a secret."

"Oh, yeah?" said Ted. "Well, I've got a secret, too." When the wheelbarrow was full, they tossed in a few spruce needles and some holly branches. "I'm going to paint the pinecones and tie ribbons on them for gifts," Patrick said.

"My *secret* is about gifts . . . gifts for someone's birthday!"

"Birthday?" Patrick echoed. "*My* birthday?"

"Maybe," Ted answered as they started back. "Listen, if you tell me your secret, I'll tell you mine."

Patrick thought for a moment. "No," he said. "I'm not telling."

During the following week, Patrick spent so much time talking about the wagon and the pushcart that he persuaded Mama Bear to go look at them. On a snowy morning they took the trolley down the hill. The flakes floating outside the windows looked like tiny ships on a sea of air; sometimes they obscured the trolley's path, then a gust of wind would blow them all somewhere else. The conductor pulled the bell and the car inched forward.

It was nearly December now, so the streets were

crowded with shoppers and Santa's Helpers stomping in the snow alongside contribution kettles for the poor. When Patrick and Mama Bear left the trolley, he tugged on her paw, making her look in every window, all of which seemed to contain diminutive worlds of speckled cotton and animated toys. From inside the shops came Christmas music and warm smells.

"Let's go look at the toys!" exclaimed Patrick. But first off, Mama Bear stopped to get tea and cocoa, then she took Patrick to the drugstore where she bought some decorations for his birthday party. At a lunch counter near the window they sat and had cream cheese sandwiches on brown bread; but Patrick couldn't concentrate. He quickly ate the middle out of his sandwich, leaving the crust, and said, "*Now* can we go look at the toys?"

Since Gilbert's was directly across the street, Mama Bear said, "I guess so."

Once inside, Patrick pulled Mama Bear to the back—there was the wagon, but the pushcart was gone! "Oh, no!" he wailed. "Somebody has bought it!"

"Well, that makes things easier, doesn't it?" she said casually. "To decide, I mean."

"I guess so," Patrick sulked. "But I really wanted that pushcart! I hope no one buys the wagon, then I won't know what to get."

Mama Bear smiled.

Just then, Patrick heard a recognizable voice, and turned to see Old Wolfgang standing before the main counter. He was asking Helga Barns for suntan lotion.

"I'm sorry, but we don't stock that in the winter," she said.

"Oh, heck!" Old Wolfgang replied.

"Hullo," said Patrick, coming over. "What do you want with suntan lotion?"

"Hullo, little bear! Tomorrow I am going south to spend the winter with my sister. I'm afraid snow is not kind to old bones. What are you up to?"

When Patrick explained that he was picking out a

birthday present, Old Wolfgang perked up. Addressing Mama Bear, he said, "Do you mind if your son comes with me for a bit?"

"Not at all," she said. "I have some shopping of my own to do. Patrick, let's meet back here in a half hour."

Elated, Patrick went off with Old Wolfgang. As soon as they were alone, the old man whispered, "You have remembered our secret?"

"Yes, I haven't told anyone—honest!"

"I knew I could trust an upstanding young fellow like you. Now another secret: When I am in the south, I will also be looking for a brand-new motor for my little carousel. If I am lucky, I'll bring it back in the spring. And then—hoo, hoo!—the animals will dance, the music will sing, and all the children will ride!"

"Oh, boy!" yelled Patrick.

"Shh! You must tell no one. It is a long time to keep a secret until I return. Can you do it?"

"Of course," said Patrick.

"Ah, good bear! I knew I was smart to trust you."

By now they had reached Old Wolfgang's house. He unlocked the door, but would not let Patrick come in. "Stay here, and I will bring a reward for your help."

Patrick waited excitedly by the door. Inside he could hear a lot of racket: things tumbling over, being shoved or lifted, and occasionally Old Wolfgang saying a bad word. There was a long spell of quiet, the door opened, and the old man appeared with a sloppily wrapped parcel. "Woola, woola . . . most disturbing! I thought I had lost it, but no, this is it." And he shoved it into Patrick's paw.

Patrick turned the parcel over, trying to figure out what it was.

"A birthday gift!" beamed Old Wolfgang. "To be opened on your birthday—not before."

"Can't you come to my party?" Patrick asked.

"Sorry. No. My train ticket is for tomorrow morning. But we shall see one another come spring." And he winked in a confiding manner.

When Patrick met Mama Bear, she looked at his parcel, gave him a sly look, and said, "Secrets again?"

"Secrets," he said.

At home, Patrick placed the parcel under his pillow. "I hope I can wait a whole week," he thought.

Patrick's birthday was the following Saturday. All that morning, Mama Bear would not let him come into the kitchen since she was busy baking and setting things up for the party, so Patrick had to remain in the parlor. He tried to read, but his mind kept straying to what kind of presents he was likely to get.

Around three o'clock, the doorbell rang, and Ted sauntered in, holding a square package wrapped in tissue paper. "Happy birthday," he called.

"Hullo, thanks," said Patrick. "I can't imagine what it is."

"You'll find out," said Ted.

Presently the other guests began to arrive: Weaver, Hanna and Maria Rinko, and last of all . . . Big Bear!

"What did you invite *him* for?" Patrick asked.

"Now, Patrick," said Mama Bear. "Be kind. It *is* your birthday."

"Yeah! You'd better leave me alone, punk!" Big Bear cried.

Mama Bear ushered everyone into the kitchen. She had moved the table to the center of the room, draped it with a yellow cloth, and arranged the chairs so that each child had a placecard with his or her name on it. Beside the cards were cups of pleated paper containing candy, and cardboard party hats with elastic bands.

Streamers were looped from the ceiling. Confetti was everywhere. "Wow!" gasped Patrick.

He sat at the head of the table, with Ted on his right and Weaver on his left. Hanna and Maria sat opposite one another, and Big Bear was placed at the far end. They all put their hats on, and Mama Bear handed round plates of ice cream. Ted squeezed Patrick's paw. "I can't wait till you see what I got you. Open mine first, O.K.?"

"O.K.," said Patrick. "Ma, can I open my presents now?"

"After we have cake and ice cream," she said.

"Darn!"

Everyone ate their ice cream up in a jiffy, but Big Bear dawdled, getting distracted, and tapping his spoon on the table, until the ice cream in his dish was just a melted puddle, and his waistcoat was covered with spills. Patrick looked at him disgustedly. "Don't let's wait for Big Bear. I want my cake!"

"Coming, coming," said Mama Bear, bringing the cake over. It was chocolate, Patrick's favorite, with his name written across the top in yellow icing.

Mama Bear solemnly lit the seven candles, turned out the lights, and everyone sang "Happy Birthday." Their faces were illuminated by the candle's orangish glow and it was an exciting moment. Mama Bear said, "Make a wish and blow out the candles."

Wrinkling his nose, Patrick thought of the best wish he could, then began to blow. Suddenly, there was another, louder blowing sound from the end of the table, and screams from Hanna and Maria. Mama Bear rushed to put on the lights.

Big Bear's melted ice cream was all over the cake, the tablecloth, the forks and spoons, and a little had splattered on the Rinko sisters.

"Gracious!" exclaimed Mama Bear. "What happened?"

"Well . . ." answered Big Bear. "You said *blow*!"

"I didn't mean you. It's not *your* birthday!" Trying to keep her temper, she got a wet dish towel and wiped up the spilled ice cream, while Hanna and Maria went to the sink to wash. All the candles on Patrick's cake were blown out. (Some were even blown over.)

"Do I get my wish anyway?" Patrick asked.

"Oh, sure," said Mama Bear.

"Stupid ox!" Ted burst out.

A scowl was crossing Big Bear's face, so Mama Bear quickly suggested that Patrick open his presents. "Wait! I almost forgot!" he said, running upstairs. When he came back, he was holding Old Wolfgang's parcel.

Patrick arranged the presents in a semicircle on the floor, then starting with Ted's, he furiously tore off the tissue paper. It turned out to be an ordinary coloring book and a box of crayons, but Ted was looking very pleased, so Patrick said, "Oh, boy! Just what I wanted!" He opened the rest of the presents just as carelessly. Weaver gave him some pickup sticks; Hanna, a game of tiddleywinks; Maria, a set of dominoes; and Big Bear, a broken Yo-Yo. Now it was Mama Bear's turn.

She left the room. There were scuffling noises, then she wheeled in a shiny mauve pushcart!

"Oh, Ma!" Patrick gasped, running over to it. "You got it after all!"

"You see," she laughed. "I can have secrets, too."

Climbing aboard, Patrick pushed down on the handle and it edged forward a few feet. "Let me try!" cried Ted.

"No, me . . . me!" Hanna Rinko screamed.

"Not in the house," said Mama Bear. So Patrick reluctantly got off. Then he remembered Old Wolfgang's parcel.

But when he undid the wrapping, Patrick saw it was only a large, blue balloon. "Darn!" he said disappointedly. "I was expecting a toy!"

"Blow it up," said Ted.

So Patrick started to blow up the balloon. He blew—and he blew—and he blew—and he blew! The balloon kept growing larger until it practically filled the room. Some things fell off the shelves, and Weaver and the Rinko sisters, afraid of being crushed, scrambled

under the table. "Stop!" cried Mama Bear. "It'll explode!"

But her warning was too late. There was a gigantic, tremendous, and deafening

and the balloon burst.

"Now you've done it!" said Ted.

But the balloon had been filled with very small toys and candy which had magically grown as Patrick blew it up, and now they came showering down like rain. Everyone ran about gathering up the prizes.

"What a wonderful balloon!" said Patrick. "This is the best birthday I've ever had!"

After all the kids had gone, he and Mama Bear stood on the stoop with the snowflakes flinging cold kisses against their faces, and looked at the cheery lights in all the houses in Puttyville brightening the night. Bringing Patrick inside, Mama Bear set him in the parlor with his new toys while she puttered round the kitchen. Later, she carried in mugs of eggnog which they sipped before the fire.

"Ma," Patrick said, "I'm very happy."

"So am I," said Mama Bear. "I'm glad you had a nice birthday."

"Oh, yes, I got everything I wanted—except for the wagon. . . . Maybe I'll get it on Christmas, huh?"

"Maybe." Mama Bear laughed. "Goodness! After Christmas is over, what will you have to look forward to?"

Patrick opened his mouth to say something, but changed his mind. "It's a secret."

Smiling, Mama Bear took up some mending, and Patrick played with his toys. From down the hill came the chime of church bells; the wind flew over the roof like reindeer, and the fire sputtered and popped. Soon Patrick's head began to nod, and he closed his eyes and fell asleep against the pushcart, dreaming of the carousel he would ride in the spring.

Format by Kohar Alexanian
Set in 12 pt. Avanta
Composed, and bound by The Haddon Craftsmen,
Scranton, Penna.
Printed by The Murray Printing Co.
HARPER & ROW, PUBLISHERS, INC.